C000227625

Originally performed at Theatro Technis in London. August 2021 with the following cast.

DANNY - Charlie Thurston
PAT - Kit Redding
THOMAS - Marcus Judd
JOHN - Archie Capon

Written two years prior.

Produced by PigPenCreative.

PigPen Creative is a daring, genre-defying theatre and film production company. Our humble beginnings in a dusty barn in Cranbrook were the catalyst for a journey that would take us through cobwebs and pockets of rust to where we are today. Driven by a desire to tell tales, we birthed dark manipulations of fairytales, absurd apple ridden takes on life, sketches, and stories.

Visit pigpencreative.com for further information.

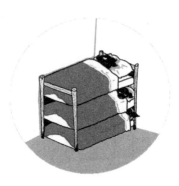

LOS TRES CERDITOS

A TRAGEDY IN ONE ACT

CHARACTERS

DANNY The oldest triplet.
THOMAS The middle triplet.
PAT The youngest triplet.

JOHN

LOS TRES CERDITOS

Lights slowly rise on a small room. Perry Como's '(There's no place like) home for the holidays plays out of a gramophone down stage right. Childlike but strangely dark harcoal etched drawings are scattered and stuck everywhere.

On the wall stage left is a huge generic poster of the Caribbean. Near it is a poster of a cat hanging off of a rope with the caption "Hang in there."

Next to the gramophone is a large bible like book with the album 'Season's greetings' by Perry Como resting on it.

A triple bunk bed is in the centre of the room and miscellaneous bits of dirty kids clothing (jackets, shirts, trousers) are scattered about the room. Empty and filled packets of space raiders are also strewn about. The bed is outlined with fairy lights badly.

A metal bucket large enough to be placed on a head sits stage left filled with bits of rubbish and stale crisps in it.

There is a large rectangular red rug on the floor with a small lump underneath.

Behind the triple bunk bed is a large chest.

At the front of the room is an old TV with its back facing the audience. Stage left and right are the same TV's, the VHS type, facing the audience.

THOMAS and PAT are lying on the carpet waiting to turn on the TV. They are both wearing one piece badly stained long johns. DANNY is in the large chest at the back of the room.

'Los Tres Cerditos' plays plays through the two screens for the audience, and the hollowed out TV on stage shines light

on the faces of the boys. The three brothers begin to act what is happening on the screen.

ALL	(*Singing*) Quién teme al lobo feroz al lobo al lobo , quién teme al lobo feroz?
PAT	En la nariz le pegaré/
THOMAS	Un nodo yo le haré/
PAT	Una patada del aire/
THOMAS	En el barro lo hundiré.

DANNY slowly emerges from the large chest and peers at the two brothers.

PAT & THOMAS	(*Singing*) Quién teme al lobo feroz al lobo al lobo , quién teme al lobo feroz?
DANNY	Abre la puerta y déjame entrar!
PAT & THOMAS	Por nada pienso dejarte entrar!
DANNY	Soplaré y soplaré y tu casa derribaré!
PAT & THOMAS	Por nada pienso dejarte entrar!

DANNY looks angry. stops his acting and stares at the brothers who are now at the back of the room.

DANNY	That's not it!

Beat.

So what, you are just going to stander over yonder and pretend you don't smell like failure.

PAT   Shut up Danny, you're wrong you necrious
                       fool.

DANNY   Am I the necrious fool? Look.

*DANNY rewinds the video to point out why they made the
mistake.*

                       Now shut it and listen... Did you repeat the
                       line? No you didn't.

THOMAS   Sorry Danny.

PAT   Sorry.

DANNY   If this happens again I will starve you both.

*The brothers all move to the front of the bed and crouch at
different heights in order of age. THOMAS picks up three
packets of space raiders, a knife, a fork and a spoon and
passes the them one by one to his older siblings. PAT gets
frustrated because he gets given the knife.*

DANNY   For food in a world where many stay in
                       hunger;

THOMAS   For faith in a world where many stay in fear;

PAT   For brothers in a world where many walk
                       alone;

ALL   Amen.

*They all begin to eat from their packets with their
implements.*

DANNY   Mam would've said something like/

THOMAS	How was your day?
PAT	Do you have much schuelly work?
DANNY	We just have to make a poster/
THOMAS	A3/ with the dibbies/ I can do them, guys.
PAT	Fine/ if i can present the words/ Danny the Dictadura as always is taking the lead bec-
DANNY	because I am the most aged of the tree of us.
PAT	Danny was ripped from mams vaginal clunch a sheer dos minutos before me, not exactly the longest time.
THOMAS	Pat we need him as the Dictadura por as a consequence we would have no drive.
DANNY	Now Mam would have butted in and cambiared the subject to something like sport/
THOMAS	Or my dibbies/
PAT	Or about Pap/
DANNY	Not about Pap/
THOMAS	Not about Pap/
PAT	Not about Pap.
Beat.	
PAT	Danny was anojised by this bully at schuelly that day

THOMAS   Danny got so anojiated you should have seen him/ his eyes were like filled with bloogree and they were red/ his oirs had steam coming from them

PAT   Like the Lobo/

THOMAS   The Lobo

THOMAS reveals a charcoal photo he drew of a wolf from his pocket. He holds it up to the audience.

PAT   Megazoom!

THOMAS stretches further so the audience can see.

DANNY   The Lobo Feroz.

PAT   Danny huffed

THOMAS   and he-

3 KNOCKS. Silence. The brothers use their utensils like weapons and THOMAS creeps towards the window.

THOMAS   (*Whispers*) Hello?

PAT   Louder.

THOMAS   Hello?!

Pause again. Brothers look at each other for a moment then continue.

PAT   Danny huffed!

PAT begins to crawl up the side of the bed onto the top bunk.

THOMAS   and he puffed!

PAT   and he grabbed the peckenny/ greasy/ filthy

THOMAS   grubby/ repugnant sweat bag of a bully/ and/

PAT is kneeling on the top bunk.

PAT   he/

DANNY   I/

THOMAS   Danny!/

PAT   struck him in the nariz/ CRACK!

THOMAS pretends to imitate the wailing of the bully as he writhes around on the carpet, minding the lump.

      Oh how he wailed and squirmed that filthy rodent raton!

THOMAS   you could hear that crack from across the playing patio/

DANNY   Oh the bloggree spat out his nariz like a can of red fly spray! HE SQUIRMED/ LOBO SYMPATHISER/ You do NOT EXASPARAR LOS TRES/ por if you DO you WILL sufrer.

PAT   I smelt the kak from the bully and I was standing mas than 5 beds away/ we smelt his fear/ the playground coal bird was celebrating with us.

THOMAS   Pat and I

PAT   We ran over and gave that Lobo
                      sympathiser one or two more for good
                      lucky.

*PAT chops with his right hand through the air, then with
his left, then balls up the energy from the air and thrusts it
forwards akin to a fireball move from an anime.*

*Whilst this happens THOMAS moves his body as to mimic
being hit by PAT.*

DANNY   The Karakus Fireball! Nice. I love you
                      brothers.

PAT & THOMAS Love you too Danny.

Brothers retire to their beds.

THOMAS   I can't dorm. Not sure why as my body has
                      that aching feel one gets when they're
                      dormy. I'll dibby instead.

                      Mam liked my dibbies, always stuck them
                      on the meat cooler, even the not so good
                      ones. Sometimes I dibby mam to see if
                      she'll pop out and say hello (he *starts to
                      draw his mother*) I can't much remember
                      her face. Slim nariz, pretty seablue eyes and
                      a smile full of teeth, just like mine (*smiles*).
                      She used to take me by my manny when I
                      was smaller. We can do that in my dibby,
                      no fermy feelings or thoughts can get us
                      from there. Maybe if I stick us up, she'll
                      pop out and say hello, maybe zum me a
                      tune and help me get to dorm.

Pause.

7

DANNY   The first line of our Libra states "A wellmannered piglet should always crecink about whether the other piglets are fermy or not, whether they are smiling or not." Since no slole cares for us piglets, we must pejiate ourselves together as one cohesive unit. We must stay tog (*he stops himself from talking and looks depressed*)

Pap was like super super strong. Probably a superhero. We used to walk through the green and he'd put me up to the blue so I could nearly touch it.

One arm scoop and id be up with the birdies. BLACKBIRD. SONG THRUSH. BLUE TIT (*laughs*) blue tit! The noble collared dove. Dad would tear across the field so fast. He'd huff and puff until his face got all thick with the warm bloogree rushing through his capillaries/ and I'd flap my armies like this. And I promesa. One time. I flew.

PAT   Can you keep a scondy? (*Giggles, runs over to snowflake light, turns it on*) I have something I shouldn't have! Back at the oregonal habitbuild I had my own dorm spot, with its own peckenny bed and dibbydesk. I didn't have to look at Danny's olourous bedmatt. Mam stegged these Amerellow resplendent stars to the ceiling and I could pretend I was in space. A spaceman, astropat! TO INFINITY AND AYOND! FIGHTER OF THE DIABLOUS SPACE RAIDERS!

Imitating holding a lazer gun with his fingers.

> ZAP!ZAP!ZAP!/

He points the snowflake light at the ceiling.

> Now I'm stuck in a glow-snobe. I don't
> much mind it/ the flakes are pretty and
> remind me of Christmas, the best time of
> year.

*THOMAS jolts upright. PAT puts on the gramophone,
Rudolph the red nosed reindeer plays. .*

THOMAS   AAAAAAAAHHHHHHHHHHHHH!!!!
IT'S TIME!!!!

ALL   IT'S TIME. TIME/ IT'S TIME/IT'S TIME!

DANNY   It's time!

*The three brothers rush to the carpet. Two lamps are placed
at the front to make it look like car headlights.*

*PAT goes through the effort of miming opening the car
door and putting his seat belt on.*

THOMAS   (*Shouting*) We are in the car...
AMARELLOW CAR! Thomas punches
Pat

PAT   Ow! Why punch me Thomas that wasn't
amarellow, that was peckenny green!

THOMAS   Haha!

DANNY   I'm sitting in the heart of the car/ Thomas
the right atrium/ Pat in the left.

THOMAS   Mam's bloogree is curdling as always/ I can
tell

PAT   Car-lights dazzle us piglets and we freeze
               like deer before being chappotted by a car
               grill.

All freeze with arms stretched out on the carpet. THOMAS
puts the gramophone on x2 speed and they double the
speed of their acting.

DANNY   Water spitting at the window

THOMAS   We are going so ruddy fast

PAT   I'm racing the gotitlets of water on the car
               window/ the car shakes/ I lose my racer.

THOMAS   ZOOM! are the cars going fast around us
               or has mam got somewhere to be?/ What if
               mam wants to bend her car around a tree
               again!?

PAT   She won't/ mam doesn't feel dark today.

THOMAS   We hope.

DANNY   My legs still ache. Like a squeeze from
               someone that won't let go. I remember this
               when the car hits the bumps.

Brothers all bump in unison.

PAT   Like the sound of the wall between our
               room and mum and pap's.

DANNY   Car windows are now sweating/ open a
               window Thomas I feel strangled

THOMAS   No I'm freezing/ also what would mam say/
               radio's playing anyways and it's mams
               favourite Christmas song.

THOMAS puts the gramophone on the slowest setting.

They all lean in to the gramophone, mesmerized, PAT snaps out of it and looks forward.

PAT   Mam's looking in the mirror, shush.

Pause whilst they all look at the rear-view mirror waiting for the mum to look away.

THOMAS   BEEP! Car races past. Mam swears.

ALL   BLEEP!BLEEP!BLEEP!BLEEP!BLEEP!

DANNY   We say nothing. Mam's words burn more bad than the lighter does.

THOMAS   I feel sick. Estomag is peckenny bit bubbly and foamy.

PAT   Thomas has gone peckenny bit green.

THOMAS   Can't be sick in mam's car.

PAT   Imagine what she would do.

DANNY   Her sneaky hands.

THOMAS   Mam is looking at me.

DANNY   Mam's looking at Thomas.

PAT   Thomas is looking at mam.

THOMAS   Frothy acid in my estomag has reached my chest. I'm gonna be sick.

DANNY   Pull the car over mam, Thomas is gonna be sick.

ALL   BLEEP!BLEEP!BLEEP!BALEEP!BLEEP
            !BLEEP!

DANNY   Mam please I don't want it on me!

PAT   Mam swears again!

ALL   BLEEP!BLEEP!BLEEP!BLEEPITY!BLE
            EP!BLEE P!BLEEP!

THOMAS   I'm ok now.

PAT   BLEEP!BLEEP!BLEEP!BLEEPITY!BLE
            EP!BLEEP!BLEEP!BLEEP!BLEEP!BLEE
            P!BLEEPITY!BLEEP!BLEEP!BLEEP!BL
            EEEEP!

PAT covers his ears, DANNY covers his eyes, THOMAS covers his mouth.

DANNY slowly puts back on the Gramophone and the three brothers start to dance around the room and put on random bits of clothing in jollity, occasionally singing sections from the song.

Once they are all dressed up in loads of clothing they move towards the door, ready to go out.

Just as PAT puts a hand on the door, they all look at each other and laugh.

DANNY and the other two brothers march from spot to spot to carry out their daily room checks.

DANNY   How is the South Wing Thomas?!

THOMAS   Spick and SPAM! Oh wait, one leak in the
            uppermost corner. Oscure spot next to it.

DANNY	Thank you Thomas! How is the North Wing looking Pat!
PAT	North Wing looking clean as a baby's whistle! Still only four leaks and two oscured spots!
DANNY	Lovely stuff (*Ticking off an imaginary list*) checking the East Wing now!... All seems in order.
PAT	West Wing is lovely jubbly!
DANNY	That's grandatious! What's the weather like today?

All look at the paradise poster on the wall.

PAT & THOMAS Another day in paradise!

DANNY   That's great!

Brothers go to their own sections of the room, waiting for the next memory.

PAT   I've gotta look smart for Holy Day gotta be radical! Blue corbatie with the amarellow stripes,white shirt, my charcoal trousers that are desgasted at the roddees and grass stained from the field yesterday. They're still wet from the rain but I gotta look smart to learn smart mam always said. Pap left the caousie already/ mam is in the kitcheena cooking breakfast and you two are in bed you lazy shits. I walks down to the kitcheena and gives mamsy an immense hug because I love her. Mam's probably crecinking about the Lobo.

It's dark out, darker than a bashed fingernail. Danny always hated the invernou winter mornings because of the dark. Mam never minded whether it was rain or shine because she was never awake enough to give a scooby, but today she was/ she must be having nochimares about him.

Looks at window. Mam screams 'Go wake your brothers up or we are gonna be late' as she's serviring up my charred pigsmeat and my huegg onto the plate. This is my task. I'm feeling radical!

I corry upstairs to Danny and Thomas and I gritout:

'WAKE UP WAKE UP WAKEY WAKEY OR YOU GUNNA BE LATEY'.

They say nothing, so I corry back down to mam because I'm hambry. Luckily my pigs meat is still hot,it's graysy saucey sweat is still sizzling and crickly crackling on my plate, now that's radical, it's a peckenny bit black though. Thomas comes in first and his hair is all funny and sticky uppy. Thomas look at your hair it's all messy! Thomas doesn't respond and he scoffs his pigs meat and hueggy like a greedy little pig.

THOMAS   Pat is being annoying and fastidious as usual. Bumlicker. BESADOR OF CULO. Mam only likes him so much because he always is the first to volunteer to help/ and because he doesn't remind her of him.

(Looks at window)

Pat's crinkled smiley face crack makes me angry. BESADOR OF CULO. Bumlicker. Mam's cooking isn't as good today, it's pants. My pigs meat is gristly, and it doesn't curl like it veccusually does. I cut my soggy huegg in dos and make two eyes with the halves and a mouth with the pigs meat. I feel virtuous. Holy Day makes me feel fermy when I crecink about it so I try not to think about the expansful castile like Holy place/ with it's golden walls and most of all the Big Cheese on the podium.

He looks a little sickened by the image.

Mam shouts 'Danny' out the door. I scrape my knife against my plate because I know that Pat hates it. Pat winces/

PAT I scrunch my face. Thomas is being a loser again. I'm still happy though. Danny COME DOWN MAM IS GETTING ANGRY!

THOMAS Mam says, 'I'm not angry Danny your food is just getting freezing and we can't be late for the Holy Day.'

PAT We *can't* be late for Holy Day.

DANNY We have Holy Day today, but I don't want to go. I can see the drizzle on my window,and I can feel the frost coming through. My legs ache from field and I feel stiff in this bed. Movement stings so I don't move. Besides my ropies are sodden from yesternochi's rain so I would have to get back into them again which is repugnantatious and makes my estomag churn pondering on it. Steps are creaking

15

up the escalares so I know I have to come up with something before mam gets here. Pull a sourface, act fermy and Mam will never know. Mam *always* knew, she was pesky like that. Her experience with the Lobo has taught her many a trick. A bit like in WarriorsRome where you complete a mission and the peckenny game scream goes. 'Baloop, new skill learnt/ double handed warrior battle chop. You also leveled up'

Danny seems lost in thinking about the game.

'Danny why don't you come eat your breakfast, your brothers are ready to go to Holy day and you haven't even cambiared.' Mam I don't wanna go/ My ropies are wet, and my legs sting, and I don't look good for the day. 'Baloop' new idea/ hairdryer down the legs to warm them up. I slip on the legs one by one. Warm. Paggy. My legs are covered in that feeling you get when you dry yourself with a towalla that's been on the radiator whilst you shower/ and it's that peckenny bit freezing perhaps in Autumn and you just feel seguridad in your towalla/ it's amazing.

PAT   You always dwell on the details that don't matter.

DANNY   Shut off

PAT   You're not supposed to do that. That's what you said.

DANNY   As if you didn't dwell either/ hyprotix.

PAT	I'm not a hyprotix/
DANNY	You are/
PAT	Not
DANNY	Are
PAT	Not
DANNY	Are
PAT	Not
DANNY	Are
PAT	Not
DANNY	ARE
PAT	NOT
DANNY	NOT!
PAT	ARE!
DANNY	WHAT?!
PAT	WHAT!
THOMAS	WE ARE IN MAM'S WOMB!

The three set up a light at the head of the carpet and they spoon on the floor in a foetal position.

DANNY	Thomas is curled next to the left fallopian tube, Pat scrunched next to the right/ my tootsies reaching up towards mam's estomag bullseye/

THOMAS	BAdump, BAdump,BAdump, BAdump
ALL	BAdump, BAdump, BAdump, BAdump
PAT	Three peckenny foetal hearts syncing to become one/ Danny move over I can't feel mam's heart thud against me/
DANNY	No it's my turn/

DANNY and PAT squirm trying to reach the light

PAT	You've felt it long enough/
THOMAS	Pat stop squidgling your cord is around my collar/

They don't stop

Stop it/ STOP!/ (*choking*)

You're strangling me!

They stop.

DANNY	We can hear the faint gritouts from mamsy/ her uterus walls are crushing us in, I'm slipping down the middle of the womb/ hold me brothers/ don't let the big DOC take me/
PAT	We won't/ hold on Danny
THOMAS	Danny your hand is reflippery/ I can't hold on!
DANNY	Mam's gritouting is getting louder and louder/ the flaps are opening/ MAM IS OPENING THE BOMBAY DOORS!

18

PAT	HOLD ON THERE DANNY/ GRAB ME TIGHTER!/ DANNY!
THOMAS	Danny is getting wrenched out by DOC/ We cant stop it/ we don't have the blogree strength to hold him/
DANNY	Plucked out into the mundy/ so bright/ my eyes can't take it-
THOMAS	Walls have shrunk again/ I'm now clunched to Pat
PAT	Nothing to clunch onto apart from each other/ grab Thomas behind his collar/ WE HAVE TO FOLLOW DANNY! DON'T HAVE FEAR/
THOMAS	DOC has Pat by the ankle/
PAT	DOC HAS ME BY THE ANKLE
THOMAS	HE TOOK PAT!

They stop for a moment and start to giggle

PAT	I like that one.
DANNY	Yeh, me too.
THOMAS	It always stops you two from quarrelling.
DANNY	(*Posh*) As Holy day is upon us/ I/ Danny Cerdito/ am allowing a peckenny siesta to rejuvenate the skin and soul.
THOMAS	(*Posh*) Danny how long doth it be.

DANNY	(*Posh*) The time shall but be decided O brother/ por my own mind and mine alone.
PAT	I don't need to dorm.
DANNY	I don't remember asking.

Brothers all go to bed for a nap.

Silence.

PAT is wide awake and looking up at DANNY's mattress.

PAT	Christmas day/ step out of my bed/ slash my tootsies on the ball ball Danny broke/ dip my fingers in the bloogree and lick it/ my bloogree/ mine/ Thomas was asleep and he
THOMAS	I wasn't asleep I was pretending to.
PAT	What are you doing awake?
THOMAS	Music woke me.
PAT	Sorry.
THOMAS	Christmas day you cut your tootsies/ I thought I would say something but I stayed hidden/ you left the habitroom/ you shouldn't have.
PAT	I leave/ go down/ bloogree prints on the white carpet/ tree looks ugly/ tree and the tinsel is malting/ shedding it's skin like a snake/ see the three presents/ looks too flat to be my ipod.
THOMAS	I know what it was/ was the disc for mams disc spinner/ rewrapped with your name on

	it/ heard it all. Laying in my bed/ hear a gritout/ hear the steps start loud then go softer/
PAT	I'm sobbing/ mam walks in and she lets loose at me/ "you're just like your bleeping brother Johnny was/ you no good/ peckenny/ naughty/ boy/ go to your room!"
THOMAS	Gritout again but this time coarser/ steps coming up/ door slams open and it's you/ watered eyes and leg bruised like a badly looked after banana.

Pause.

You mustn't blame yourself for what Jo. The Lobo caused. We are in this as Los Tres/ forever.

He holds out his pinky

Pinky Promesa.

They interlock pinkies and smile.

Nochi.

PAT	Nochi.

Lights go down and back up.

DANNY sits upright.

DANNY	Arise young piglets the Holy Day hath arrived.

The piglets awake, put on something that resembles a suit and they march three times around the bed. DANNY makes a pulpit out of whatever is in the room.

	The church walkway is expanding in front of us/ eeeelooooongaaaatinggg forwards and forwards
THOMAS	I feel like Luigi in SuperMario64 23 June 1996 edition/ when he just gets engulfed in the castile doors/ opens up/ pixels pretty as paps painting over my dibbies used to be when he cared/ princess peach was my favourite/ peachyweachy...
PAT	No!/ Goomba gumbo/ he's so funny/ just when you-
DANNY	ENOUGH!/ us tres piglets idling at the far side of the walkway/ we are so peckenny we can fit in mam's body shade
THOMAS	The big Holy man/ we can just about see him
PAT	His silhouette marked out against the pretty Holy walls/
DANNY	He's the Big Cheese round where we dwell/
THOMAS	The large kahuna/
DANNY	Head honcho/
THOMAS	Top dog/
PAT	The Holy One.

DANNY

Shuffling onto our pews/ I can view a sea of familiar faces/ we know what they're all crecinking/ they're crecinking about him.

Points at the window. All their heads slowly fixate on the window.

PAT

Fuzzbeard is your classico case of a bystander up to no good on Holy day/

DANNY

Yeh! I've seen him churn out his sins in the confession cube more times than I can count/

THOMAS

Or what about Sonic/ what's she up to

PAT

She's called sonic because of her spikey azlue coloured hair

DANNY

It's ridiculocious

PAT

I crecink it's pretty cool actu-

THOMAS

The hymn!/ Abide with me, fast falls the eventide;

ALL

The darkness deepens Lord, with me abide; When other helpers fail and comforts flee; Help of the helpless, oh, abide with me.

DANNY

Thomas Cerdito/ is there anything you wish to confess?

THOMAS

No your honor.

DANNY

Patrick Cerdito/ is there anything you wish to confess?

PAT hesitates for a moment.

PAT   No your honor.

DANNY   I hereby declare I have nothing to confess either.

In the room adjacent (either on stage or in the audience) JOHN is revealed wearing a white polo neck and a black overcoat. Black umbrella in his right hand. He jumps up onto a chair.

The three brothers are watching 'Los Tres Cerditos' in their room in silence in their respective bunks the audio is not playing but the video feed still comes through faded.

JOHN   I'M ON THE TIPPITY TOP OF DA FUCKING WORLD/ LIKE KING KONG ON THE EMPIRE STATE! JOHNNY HAS GOT HIS JAMBO/ TOOK A WHILE THOUGH DIDN'T IT (*laughs*) Was conceived and I told me mamsy she was wrong to bring me into da world/ too many problems/ UNLESS YOU ARE AT THE TIPPITY TOP THAT IS!/ Mamsy's a slut isn't she!/ can twiddle and fiddle with her thumbs and cause some real mischief/ DID YOU KNOW MAMSY HAS BEEN AT IT WITH THE POSTYMAN AGAIN?!

I spoke with PAPSY/ He comes running in/ He screams his soul at me like he does/ for my papsy he lacks that restraint a father really should have nowadays/

"OI SON YOUR MAMSY BEEN AT IT AGAIN WITH THE POSTY MAN" or something like that. I KNOW I WAS THERE, MAMSY DON'T THINK I KNOW THIS STUFF BUT I DO/

MAMSY'S A SLUT/ she got those wandering hands don't she the harlot! WENCH!

"DON'T YOU SPEAK ABOUT YOUR MOTHER LIKE THAT"

DO ONE OLD TIMER/ GO BACK TO WORK/ I DON'T HAVE TIME TO WORRY ABOUT THIS STUFF WHEN I'M AT THE TIPPITY TOP OF DA FUCKING WORLD

Pause.

"I need to tell you something son"

HURRY UP THEN/ I'm about to miss my 11:45 with the attractive bike from the education prison.

Beat.

"Son your mamsy is pregnant with triplets, you are gonna be a big brother, so no more shit around the house"

Pause.

I stop and think.

CHRIST ALIVE!/ the slag will inflate over the next few months/and with all the wrong beginnings/ could pop her with a sharpened chopstick or something. I tell my pap to fuck off and he does. I stop again...Three brothers. My brain is melting again/ I'm sitting on my sofa thinking...FUCK!/ I look into my future/ pap/ mamsy/ three little ones screaming their fucking skulls off, stealing my limelight/ over my rotting corpse they'll steal my Johnny jambo. BUGGER THIS!/ I'm a tell my mamsy that she's wrong to bring any more into this rotted cesspit. I have to stop her from making the same mistake twice! Snap open my door, grab my overcoat/ window is sodden wid sky sweated sadness so I decide it's best I bring my umbrella/ open the door/ sprint up the street and freeze...

Pause.

FORGOT MY RUDDY STUFF!/
STUPID FUCKER

JOHNNY/ run back to my wardrobe/ grab some playing cards/ my lucky two marbles and a coathanger. I'm running down the street once more. 4:30PM and it's already dark. Love the winter/ no one can ever see me/ think about fog/ think about the tear gas/ think about tears.

Smile.

Postyman lives just up the street. I'm sweating/ throat tastes like blood like I been swallowing glass/ shredded. Postyman been too busy shagging my mamsy and not cutting his turf it seems/ all scraggly and overgrown/ maybe he likes it all overgrown and wild/ I giggle to myself and think of mamsy. Kick his fucking door in.

Brothers react to the knock next door.

THRAP. MAM! MAM! MAM! "What do you want son". Mam, Pap told me what you done. Hence I am at Postyman's house not ours. Come down mam. A Standoff/ mam top off the stairway/ towel round her titties and vag/ Postyman behind. YOU CAN FUCK OFF! He stays. Fine. Real western stand-off.

Mam has the high ground. House smells

like burnt toast and mams shitty cheap perfume.How cliche. How could you mamsy? Come down mamsy. Stepping/ creaking at me/ creaking a real shrill tone making my neck spasm like that tick I had as a kiddy/ mams real close. Grab her neck and pull her/ rip her towel off and thrust my coat hanger up her sneaky and bedraggled snatch. Screaming in her face/ she's scraping at mine/ Postyman comes running down/ a full six and a half inch kitchen cutter comes thrashing down on my neck ending it all too soon/ just enough time to see my mamsy's blood wet face squeal before the lights go out.

The lights go out.

Long silence.

The lights did come back on as fast as they went out though, no way they gonna be taking me that easy. Sometimes think this is hell/ but it can't be/ having way too much fun. I got my responsibilities anyways. I'll digress. One thing sort of fell on top of the other and before I knew it I was back being that normal cheeky Johnny with about half of his jambo. Mamsy and Papsy wanted nothing to do with Johny Jambo but that/ is/ no/ matter! Foster friends is what came next. Yes the parents is there but they was by no means the best bit/ that being me second mamsy had some knockers/ by knockers I mean huge jiggly juggies but Papsy 2 would get all aggy when I ogled so I learnt to keep my eyes to myself/ only when he wasn't looking though HAHA. Me and the foster friends got up to some real good mischief. You lot should've been there/ was nuts/ started with a bit of casual skating/ and you know how that goes/ casual bit of skating turns into a casual bit of shoplifting AHAHAH!

One times I was just-

John can hear the brothers next door, he stops dead in his tracks and starts to hyperventilate.

THOSE CHEEKY FUCKING CHEEKY/ CHEEKY/ NASTY LITTLE FUCKING SO/ AND/ SO'S

JUST INTERRUPTED MY FUCKING STORY!/ I am so sorry little ones let me just give them ungrateful fuckers a little fright. Where was I? UGH! Doesn't matter/ Oh no! My foster friends HAHA. SO there was me/ Johnny fucking Jambo/ aka the Supreme leader/ I was the boss/ and me hunchies was Fred and Ed/ at least that's what I called them! We used to do this thing/ we knew this girl right/ name was/-

28

DOESN'T MATTER WHAT HER
FUCKING NAME IS YOU NOSEY
BASTARDS!

Us three night monsters crawling up my
foster street. ARROWHEAD
FORMATION! You know how it goes
you cheeky girl!(*winks badly*) God I can't
wink for shit/ another tale there don't you
worry girly/ I'll come back to it. You see
Fred used to carry round his pet rock or
some complete loser thing like that and me
and Ed/ (*posh*) Ed and I! We decided it
was best he let go of little stoneywoney/ He
said no way Johnny Jambo that is my pet/
Ed slapped him and called him a rock
fucker. HILARIOUS. Fred started shouting
I aint a rock fucker that isn't true/ I says
"well Freddy Fred Fred, if that is most true
then throw the thing through LindyLoo's
window up there". LindyLoo was the
Rapunzel of my foster street/ the things I
would have done to be strangled by her
hair. Lushus type/ bet she uses tresemme or
something fancy/ we loved her/ but poor
missy Rapunzel's window was about to get
hittywittyed by stoneywoney! (*laughs*) I'm
laughing just thinking of it. So soft Fred after
some gentle persuading decided he would
throw stoneywoney. Leans back/ can smell
his profuse sweating from couple steps
away/ his face glistening/ dirty young thing/
can't stand filth like that/ slow motion he
throws his stupid fucking pet stone at the
window! Rapunzel screams and we dash/
but I can't get enough can I? Always
wanting more.

Now the best bit/ this genius little tactic I have been using in the modern day I will have you know. Couple days later I went without my two hunchies to Rapunzel's window. You see it still has the crack in it she can't afford to have the pane replaced, I would give her pain alright brilliant/ clamber up her drain pipe/ got me thinking bout her fallopians/hollow/ wowzer/ Johnny's johnny now has a little jambo too HAHA! Get close enough to the window and I whispers through it. "Rapunzel Rapunzel, why don't you let down your tresemme hair you cheeky blonde." I slide back down the pipe and hide in the bush. ABSOLUTELY FUCKING BRILLIANT! Her stupid/ puny face pressed up against her mossy window looking scared fucking shitless. Bit cold out but a good prank never failed to warm anyone up.

DANNY   I sponder wether it's raining outside.

PAT   (*Looking at the paradise poster over the window*)

What do you mean, it's a wonderful day?

DANNY   I crave that happy gloopy feeling the rain gave me when I lingered in it for too long.

DANNY says nothing

I liked it when I was thrust into the shower even though I basically just had one outside. I crecink it is raining outside.

For food in a world where many stay in hunger;

THOMAS	For faith in a world where many stay in fear;
PAT	For brothers in a world where many walk alone;
ALL	Amen

The brothers all go to bed.

JOHN has his ear pressed up against the window. Three brothers are in their beds.

DANNY	Is there something you want to tell us Pat?
PAT	Huh?
DANNY	You had the chance to tell us anything in the confession box/ but you chose to lie.
PAT	What are you talking about Danny.

DANNY picks up the snowflake light and thrusts it in PAT's face.

PAT says nothing.

DANNY	Get in.
PAT	Make me.
THOMAS	Pat/ listen to Danny.
PAT	No!
DANNY	I am getting seriously sick and fermy of you! You said promesa you would trust me. You just going to throw that away like you have no morals. Necrious piglet. Get in the habitroom.

PAT gets in the habitroom. DANNY begins to recite the rules.

	A well mannered piglet should always crecink about whether the other piglets are fermy or not, whether they are smiling or not.
THOMAS	The mealtimes are there to keep us straying from hunger. (*pointing at the large book*) Our Libra is there to make the piglets stay well behaved.
DANNY	A scared piglet is a sensible piglet. We watch the vision for fun and for learning. It is super important we ejertise or we will all stop being smiley. The Libra says that all of these things are important, and if any crockoed peckenny piglet fucker sins against it then he knows what will happen to him.

He points towards Pat in the habitroom.

THOMAS	Our jobs are important. Fun is also important so we will relax to the disc-spinner or the vision.
DANNY	If a piglet was to oink over the music then that piggy would also be sinning, but in another way. A way that would make my eyeswet and my bloogree boil. But a perfect piggy always pardons a piglet that makes a silly error, with a peckenny punishment.

DANNY sighs and looks sick of reciting the same thing over and over.

PAT   (*from the box*) NECRIOTIC FLESH
SACKS.

I'M WELL AWARE OF YOUR OLIOUS
RULES AND METHODS OF LIVING. I
READ THE SAME LIBRA AS YOU.

*DANNY kicks the box a few times violently then lets PAT
out. Pat emerges, clearly shaken.*

PAT   I'm sorry

DANNY Nochi.

PAT & THOMAS Nochi.

The brothers go to bed.

JOHN   The punishment box/ nice/ a favourite of
mine in fact. They got that idea from good
old mamsy. Mamsy mamsy mamsy/ she'd
be all like. "Johnny you haven't made your
bed!" or "Johnny you can't do such nasty
things to your classmates" blahdy blahdy
blah. "Get in the cupboard Johnny or I'll tell
your papsy". Jokes on her, I like it in there/
I hid me bloody pokemons in there so I
could play/ until mam started interrupting
with the fly spray spurting and squirting
under the door and what have you. Tryna
choke me out/ monster/ somewhat
impressive you have to give it to old mamsy.
Tell you what/ I'll show you one of my
prankies. Bored of watching them lot now/
time for a cheeky
Johnnyjambomysteryprankospecial.

JOHN knocks on the window gently

(*Whispering*) Hello? Hello? Why don't you come over and let me smell your wonderful hair oh stranger.

JOHN begins to giggle.

DANNY is startled and scared by the noise. He quietly gets of his bed and moves towards the window.

This isn't as good as I imagined it/ I can only hear the bastard/ Rapunzel's reaction was way better than this/ no matter. (to the window) Why don't you remove that picture you got hanging your side/ then I can get a better look at you/ don't be frightened/ it's just Johnny Jambo.

JOHN giggles again, DANNY stays frozen

Forgive me friend/ As a fellow neighbour I have but noticed some significant quarrelling emanating fr-

DANNY   Yyyou aa

JOHN   Do not be afraid neighbour.

DANNY   Lobo.

JOHN   Lobo?

DANNY   You don't sound like the vision does.

JOHN   You've got me all wrong son/ I'm Johnny Jambo.

Pause.

Johnny Jambo, You know?/ Sir Johnny Jambo/ most brave knight of the four kingdoms/ Let me tell you a tale, long ago, before your young self was born/ I travelled over the seven tumultuous seas to meet a tyrannical leader in Ethelhelm. He had rained terror for fourty a year and the people were but suffering you see. The leader's name was Ivag the Ruthless. Oh he was a most terrible man/ forgéd in the fiery pits of hell. A ravenclaw had sent a message to yours truly, written by most fine a maid who Sir Johnny Jambo, spoiler alert, unsheathed his monstrous sword for haha which read, Dear Sir Johnny Jambo, you must but come and save our people yadyadayada. I arrived and I slayed Ivag the Ruthless with th

DANNY   *(Quietly)*

With the glowing dagger of Athasgor/ acquired from the peckenny town seis months before.

JOHN   You heard the story? Word doth but travel fast.

DANNY   It's from a videogueg I played called Warrio

JOHN   WarriorsRome? For fucks sake/ those damned corporations.

I told them specifically not to create the game because it ruins the myth/ what I accomplished was greater than what a few pixels could create.

35

DANNY	How do I know you are not telling menties.
JOHN	Telling menties? Kid what are yo
DANNY	How can I trust you.
JOHN	I have something that proves it.
DANNY	Show me.
JOHN	Well one/ why would I give my most sacred possession to you/ and two, you would just tell your silly little brothers over there.
DANNY	No that's injusticeful.
JOHN	That's not even a fucking word.
DANNY	Don't swear.
JOHN	What you gunna fucking do/ I'm Sir Johnny Fucking Jambo of the
DANNY	Be tranquil! (*Quiet*) I won't tell them. Show me.
JOHN	You see that's the thing, it's a special object that had this spell cast upon it.
DANNY	An amulet.
JOHN	Yes if you like. And this
DANNY	Amulet
JOHN	Are you gunna let me fucking talk.

Pause.

Thank you. Now this amulet has a special spell cast upon it/ a spell that does not allow it to leave this room.

DANNY   I can just gaze at it through the window.

JOHN   Maybe you could/ but you need to hold it to feel the power.

JOHN stands up and stares at the window.

Take down the poster you have that side.

DANNY   No.

JOHN   I knew a child like you once. Funny little fellow/ He obviously knew me because I am Sir Johnny Jambo the Great/ so he comes running up all like "Johnny johnny" That's Sir Johnny Jambo to you, you little squeedle. "Sorry Sir Johnny" He was all like wanting to be as great as me. "Ooh Sir Johnny tell me how to be so brave" and whatnot. I say "Very well my little Squire, but before you can be brave/ my squire/ dear boy/ you have to renounce your wretched parents, cast them away like a stone to sea for no true great man can reach the top without a sufficient certain sacrifice. Sir Johnny Jambo the oh so Great was not always 'oh so Great', he too had to cast aside his useless possessions to reach the tippity top. The child disobeyed your faithful Johnny Jambo and his parents did but squander their rations and the boy starved to death three months later. So the moral of the story is always listen to Sir Johnny Jambo.

DANNY gets up and slowly begins to peel away the poster.

> There's a good little lad. It'll be back up in
> no time. Just clamber through and once
> you're through we can stick it back up so
> not to startle your brothers if they wake.

DANNY begins to clamber through. They both try to stick the poster back up from their side.

THOMAS jolts upright from a sleeping position.

THOMAS   AAAAAAAAHHHHHHHHHHHH!!!!
IT'S TIME!!!!

PAT & THOMAS IT'S TIME. TIME/ IT'S TIME/IT'S TIME!

Two brothers try to form the car but realise DANNY is not there.

PAT   Oh look at this! Demands me to the
habitroom yesternochi and that same
mongulous toad is dwelling and chilling on
the top bunk/ up on his mighty castile made
of wood/ ohh the i-ron of it all.

THOMAS   He may not be feeling well.

PAT   I'll be the judge of that! Danito/ Danny!
Danny? Thomas. Thomas! Get up here!

PAT is shocked.

THOMAS   What is it? Is he O.K? Pat?

PAT does not respond. THOMAS looks and sees that DANNY is not there he begins to hyperventilate.

PAT	Our brother has been robbed by the Lobo.
THOMAS	He can't have been robbed Pat/ we are in the brick!
PAT	Well obviously he can/ he isn't here. I just crecink-
THOMAS	What are we going to do Pat? Pat? Pat?!
PAT	Won't you just shut up and let me crecink!

PAT paces the room a few times

We are in the car!

THOMAS doesn't respond or continue the memory.

WE ARE IN THE CAR!

THOMAS	AMARELLOW CAR!
PAT	Ow! Why punch me Thomas that wasn't amarellow, that was peckenny green!
THOMAS	Haha!

PAT shifts over to THOMAS' position and says his lines.

PAT	I'm sitting in the heart of the car/ Thomas the right atrium/ Pat in the left.
THOMAS	Mam's bloogree is curdling as always/ I can tell
PAT	Carlights dazzle we piglets and we freeze like deer before being chappotted by a car grill.

Pause as the brothers look at each other trying to remember the lines.

Water spitting at the window!

THOMAS   We are going so ruddy fast

PAT   I'm racing the gotitlets of water on the car window/ the car shakes/ I lose my racer.

THOMAS   ZOOM! are the cars going fast around us or has mam got somewhere to be?/ What if mam wants to bend her car around a tree again!?

PAT   She won 't/ mam doesn't feel dark today.

THOMAS   We hope.

PAT   FUCK!FUCK!FUCK!FUCKING!NECR IOUS!FUCKI NG!FOOL!/ YOU FUCKING NECRIOUS FOOL

Runs over and starts to hit the wall

DANNY!FUCKING DANNY DANNY FUCKING DANNY!FUCK!FUCK!OLIOUS FUCKING FUCK!YOU HAVE ARUANED US/ FORSAKEN FUCK!

DANNY can hear the knocking on the wall and begins to worry, before he can fully start to stress JOHN runs and puts on Wagner on his music player.

JOHN   I tell you what my young squeedlet/ you need to learn a thingy or two about manners.

DANNY	I know manners like the back of my wrist/ you can't teach this peckenny piglet a thing.
JOHN	From now on you speak not the tongue of your realm/ you speak the tongue of the Jambo

JOHN scrambles for a word.

Jambinish! My language/ not yours/ none of this 'peckenny' or 'pig' nonsense.

Attention! I said attention! You move your legs together like this and stand up straight and salute Sir Johnny Jambo and say "Yes Sir Johnny Jambo Sir!" ATTENTION!

DANNY tries to imitate what JOHN did and fails

You inbred squeedlet/ fucking oaf/ loaf of banana bread/ in bread. HAHA that is fucking funny. ATTENTION!

DANNY	Yes Sir Johnny Jambo Sir!
JOHN	There's a good little squeedle! Now I want you to read this/ you see the highlighted bits?
DANNY	Um yes.
JOHN	They are yours/ Do not fucking read the other bits.
DANNY	(*reading poorly*) Oh Sir Johnny Jambo, I
JOHN	Did I tell you to start?!

DANNY   Sorry Joh Sir Johnny Jambo.

*PAT and THOMAS sit in silence for a while, lost as to what
they should to. PAT gains an idea.*

PAT   Thomas go back/ down the escalares from
               your habitroom, past paps no entry zone
               and through the kitcheena/ standing at least
               three beds altall is

THOMAS   The Libra shelf/ the home biblary/ millions
               of unused peckenny libras

PAT   Yes/ remember the libra/ middle shelf,
               hustled in between paps libra about Wayne
               Roonman I crecink and the other one about
               the great war? Pap was a stickler for an
               information libra.

THOMAS   I know the one.

JOHN   HOW MANY BLUEBERRIES IN A
               MULBERRY TREE!

DANNY   TWOTY THREE

JOHN   SIR JOHNNY JAMBO'S MULBERRY
               TREES ARE!

DANNY   JUST THE RIGHT MULBERRY SHAPE
               FOR YOU AND ME!

JOHN   WHERE DOES MY LOVE WAIT AND
               PONDER!

DANNY   BY THE MULBERRY TREE OVER
               YONDER!

JOHN   YES! NOW!

The two take a moment to compose themselves

DANNY   Oh Sir Johnny Jambo my love, I was so scared but my heart 'twas sunk/ How rain sets early in this night/ Wind snatches branches from their trunk/ But you my love are here in might/

JOHN   *(to the audience)* Now does Rapunzel fine and fair/ Glide through my door and shun the wind/ So long and lush her tresemme hair/ Desire burns bright, our souls are twinned.

Pause.

                  So much better. The Orcmen by Gwendleford will be pleased with you.

DANNY   Send them my regards Sir Johnny.

JOHN   FUCKING TITS!/ 12 O' CLOCK/ Draconids, I'm now rushing the right flank with the pearl of Evermore

DANNY   Left flank inaccessible due to peckenny bit of floo-

JOHN punches DANNY

JOHN   You little egg always going back to your sullied roots.

DANNY   Sorry Sir

JOHN   No you ruined it, always fucking ruining it/ naughty squeedle, I'm upset now.

DANNY   Don't be like that

Grabs JOHN's hand and places it on his hair.

               Just hold on to me for a minute.

PAT   An elong elong elongated period in the past
               were two peckenny beauties/ one male

THOMAS   One female/

PAT   One with her womb/

THOMAS   One with his sword/

PAT   (*to the audience*) this is one of those super
               elong elongated periods ago where magia is
               as common as gloop/ the boticaranist was a
               habitbuild where many could buy their
               esters/ brebajes and potions.

THOMAS   The female was named Poppyra, and was
               part of one clan called the Pyramies.

PAT   The male was named Robert and was part
               of another called the Thesps.

*THOMAS clambers up onto the top bunk and dangles his
legs over the edge.*

THOMAS   I HATE MY OLIOUS FLIPPING
               NAME/ Poppyra Poppyra/ pap why could
               you not have named me something different/
               bloogree scoundrel my pap/ Pyramies are
               known for their slashing and chappotting
               and machitting and so on and so forth/i'm
               sitting in my habitroom on the fortyfroth
               floor of an apartment block and i'm
               crecinking about bloogree boys/ it's always

about a bloogree boy isn't it/ I like those one's with the big peches and biceps/boys make the marvellous mundy go around/ talking about going round I'm looking at my fan rotating and rotating and rotating and rotating, slowly/ the damn thing is malfunct, probably due to the fact I chapotted it with my head to see if I could make it through/ The maid is passed out in the bañotub so it's just peckenny Poppyra on her swoony todd/ as per usual. Getting sweaty in this habitroom so I better rush and open my window/ window swings open and OH MY WORD a dazzling dolop of splendour hits my peckenny eye/ bicicling across the italian waterway side/

PAT   I'm basically the kneesbees/ my thighs are dwoling from how fast i'm pedaling my bici, skin and cloth are as sodden as a wind turbine the sea version because the damn sun is beating me with its hot poker.

I got to keep a keen eye out for any pesky peckenny Pyramie that trundles a gammy leg onto my turf/ ROBERTS

TURF/ STAY BACK ALL CHALLENGERS/

sometimes I trundle my own leg onto the turf of the Pyramies just to show them who's the capitan/ I'm the capitan/ I don't need a leeder/ I don't need someone to tell me what to do! I'm taking my bici and I'm peddling and peddling/ I'm peddling to find the dragon/ puntuigged toothed monster/ melts people like an oversized firelighter/ melts them right down to the huessycress/

leaves them crusty/ carcinogenic toast/ you should have seen th

THOMAS   Velociating down the endless azlue ceiling/ DRAGON!/ *(imitating a dragon)* wings estretched out wide/ scabby scales blocking the light of the sun/ a solar eclipse but with a dragon. He's oscillating and careening back and yonder/ upforth and downward/ He's going for my fine leggéd biciclist/ escupitting flames from his nasal caves.

PAT   The firey pigeon/ wingéd furnace/ you hath finally come/ I unsheath my sword/ my bloogree is listo and firm/ my wingéd counterpart dives

PAT rolls out of the way.

                Better luck next time necrious dragon!

THOMAS   The flying terror is going round for a second poke, this time lower/ a lanzad of molten clay is ejecting from it's gullet/ demonic claws primed and at the ready.

PAT   AGHHHHHH!

THOMAS   AHHHHHHH! The beast is morid! But my peddling prince/ he has but been engulfed in the flames?! No, he's fine/ but wounded/ I must go and help.

THOMAS goes over to tend to PAT.

PAT   Lights are fading/ life is corrying away from me.

JOHN   I tell you what my young squeedle/ I think
                tonight is the night/ No no! Tonight is the
                night!/ just imagine/ the lights are beaming
                down, them spectators are cheering our
                names/ Who's that? I see someone famous
                in the crowd/ They've come to see Sir
                Johnny fucking Jambo and his well trained
                squeedle! Oh it's fucking wonderous/ they
                can sense the jambo that us two have got/
                can't they? can't they?

DANNY   Yes Sir.

JOHN   Aren't you glad you dropped those
                cancerous 'siblings' that you squatted with/
                no no, I don't want to talk about it/ makes
                me sick thinking about it/ can't think about
                it... aren't you glad you are now sitting with
                the best performer and knight/ Sir Johnny
                Jambo?! (*excited*) Go on! Open the box/
                it's time/ it's for you!

DANNY opens the box inside is a dress and some makeup.

                Oh tonight is going to be just perfect! Just
                perfect! I'm telling you!

DANNY starts to get dressed.

PAT   Alas she cured me with her humid mannys,
                but from those same mannys I am snatched.

                She fights for the Pyramies/ she saw my
                Thespian badge but she cured me still/
                oiring such repugnantatious news stings my
                heart/ deep deep down/ her face resembles
                a love I always had but never obtained/ a
                love that no one ever gave me/ empty life
                without her/ forbidden living with her/ what

is my mundy without this newly found significance. My Thesp ally should not have robbed my dull body from her curing enganch. Looking up at the Loon affirms my pensivity; I would rather I was morid cold/ than festering in a maggot mundy crippled by the absence of love.

THOMAS   I should have known he was a Thesp. Tyrannical Thesp but with the face of Gabriel. The loon fixates on my window this nochi/ and I can't help but feel it connects our hearts and minds/ mexcling into one glow that illuminates our bleak antiparidise. This nochi I shall send a coal bird with a note attached, The note shall say: "Sitting under this cold beamed loon, a dangerous thought has started to swell,

PAT   My mente will not lay tranquil until our eyes can fix one mas time meet down by the river this nochi, our flesh shall fundir into one. Yours truly, Poppyra."

DANNY   I sit within the walls of a beast's lair, So high, so far the eye can reach yet still It is no more than a dead photograph. Upon this tower no smell tickles my neb, No smell of dew or freshly budded bloom. Rotted wood wall. Rancid mildew and moss. Tonight if the lack of cloud permits me, I shall stare up at the star doodled shapes That dot themselves in plenty round earth's shell, Dreaming of a moment where I smell dew. Dreaming of a past that I never had. Longing for a life where I could have lived.

JOHN   Sat on my steed which is gallant and quick, I tear the fields of Ethelhelm to find My

48

love; I hear she dwells on ground most high,
With hair dangled so clean out of her cage,
For days I'll search, to find my girl up high,
My girl most high, much higher than the rest.
The lady that will treat me right this night,
All nights, all days, my years will have more
zest. No more hours of torment, strife and
grief. A fine maiden to make my life less
drab, Reading me tales of affection, I smile,
I ponder, what would my life have been If I
always had that someone who cared.

PAT   Pacing up the river side/ the air lacks gust
and is rotten with the stench of pescal
carcass/ carcasses that are fudging into the
riversand. Pyramies are setting go artificial
fire bangers into the endless ceiling in
celebration of their victory over the Thesps.
Zancudies are zapping and zibbing over the
rivers flatish head, darting at bare skin/
longing to puncture my flesh with their
puntuigged hypodermic needles that grow
out their insectal scalps, wishing to suck and
suck and suck and drain out my bloogree
until I am no more. FIVE PYRAMIES
RACING UP THE RIVER'S BANK/
except they have no swords in their hand/
no weapon to battle/ just five smirks. My
heart feels like a surgeon has just machitted
it with his rubber glove/ chappotted the
arteries connected to my pulmonaries and
my vena cava, then left it to supperate on
the countertop. In one of the Pyramies right
hand, Poppyra's Rolling Stone's teeshirt/ the
one with the labes and the teeth/ with the
lengua protruding out like this (*sticks out
his tongue*), bloogree all over/ covered/
drenched. They drop it and dash/ back
down the river's side.

49

The crecought of the blood that this grandious universe gave to me/ sullied and corpsed by some 'greater fucking being'. People are nothing but ephemeral flickers of a constantly dying flame/ the smallest gust and your out for the count. One minuto you are gliding high on a 'candidity' that your loved one gave you and promesaed/ the next you are back writhing in the mud from whence you fucking came. Whence I came sounds nice.

THOMAS   Those pesky pyramies stole my Rolling Stones tour of 82/ I am sprinting down to the river so rapid my knee junt feels like it's gonna chappot.

Pat picks up a plastic bag and places it over his head and suffocates himself

I'm gasping for the fresh summer air like nobody's business. I'm following the trail of resplendent stars/ leading me towards my Robert/ I'm connecting the dots as I corry/ thinking about mam and the connect the dots libras she gave me Oh bugger that's not in the story sorry Pat. Oh well, sod it/ makes me creink about that time at the old caousie/ Pat you remember that time we were on mams squishy sofa/ with that connecting the dots book/making piglets out of the lines you make between the dots-

Silence for a moment. THOMAS notices PAT unmoving on the floor.

Pat?

THOMAS has a moment of silence. He hugs his brother upright and realises he is dead. Still hugging he removes the bag from PAT's head and places it over his.

DANNY   Alas! Over yonder wheatfield side A steed gallops and pants its way to me. Atop sits a

DANNY stops himself and starts to huff and puff.

                    I can't do this anymore... I can't do this anymore.

JOHN   What do you mean you can't do this anymore, rotten squeedle take it back. Take it back. TAKE IT BACK. You're always laughing, all of you. They left me, they/they fucking left me cold and you all laughed,they strung me/ hooked up high by the ankles, my wrists, my thin veins slit wide open, hot blood gushing out onto the icy slaughterhouse floor with you all/ fucking/ laughing. THIS IS NOT FOR YOU TO TAKE AWAY DANNY. This is not for you to take away.

DANNY strikes JOHN, removes his wig and starts to strangle him with it.

DANNY   You sebotious villain/ your bloogree veins ooze negrish gunk. Mam left you to stagnate on your swoony for a razon and that razon I now realise. Make me leave my brothers! MAKE ME SPIT YOUR TONGUE! I DANNY CERDITO SENTENCE YOU LOBO TO INFINITY IN THE INFERNAL FUCKING PITS OF HELL! I hope your eyes liquify in the heat/ and that your hair burns so strong you smell the zapped fly like odour of it/ I want to see the

51

moscas try and crawl from the sockets of your face as you lay/ depleting to absolutymently nothing/ "Squeedle" this/ "squeedle" that/ you are a peckenny lump of pathetic flesh and I want nothing to do with you. You do not tell me what to do for I am THE ELDEST OF LOS TRES! STAY OUT OF OUR MUNDY! I'm going back to my brothers and I'm making life normal. Untouched and unsullied. You do not touch me or my fucking brothers again you oir me? For a perfect piggy always ends a piglet that makes a silly error, with a peckenny punishment/ except in your case you are finished/ finito/ fucked! YOU DO NOT/ EXASPARAR/ LOS/ TRES/ POR/ IF/ YOU/ DO/ YOU WILL SUFRER!

JOHN is dead.

DANNY takes a moment, staggers towards the window and climbs through it to see his two lifeless brothers.

He panics and lets out a pained groan. He stares forwards, turns around.

DANNY   Arise young piglets for the holy day hath arived!

DANNY scrambles and turns on the TV. The final credits of the cartoon are about to begin. He hugs his two dead brothers, opens the habitroom revealing four childhood pictures, one for each brother, the one of John crossed out, dressed up in Halloween costumes, smiling.

He gets in the habitroom and closes himself in.

CURTAIN

Printed in Great Britain
by Amazon